YEAR 2059

Transmutation

Naif Makmi

Cover Design by: Andriy Dankovich.

ISBN-13: 978-1-73-673045-4 (Paperback
format)

Author: Naif@naifbooks.com

www.naifbooks.com

Philippa:
A self-driven astrobiologist whose main motivation centered on protecting her brother Danny, from harm's way.

Ork:
An ambitious extraterrestrial and mastermind who repeatedly destabilizes the earth, in a bid to overrun and override the humans and Elk's tribe of aliens.

Chapter One

COHABITANTS

Earth had received it's long expected visitors. Before they had entered the earth's sphere, they had signaled
for permission, following all the gestures atypical to the non-intrusion of airspaces.

It was a spaceship of aliens from the remotest parts of the galaxy. They did not land in the ocean as was typical to parachuted capsules but amidst a location reserved for some of the activities of man.

Finally, aliens were on the earth and they had come in peace. Answering some of the first questions, they assured the world that they didn't plan to tactically and overtly colonize the earth as was long suspected of extraterrestrials. They claimed they had no such interests in overriding the events of a foreign planet.

They had envisioned earth to be the most incubating of planets in the solar system. But if the forms of life therein, or the essence thereof, they hadn't paid sufficient attention to.

They were resettled and cohabited two cities with humans as a really small tribe of aliens. They spread themselves into two cities for strategic reasons to them, which was yet unknown to the humans. In time, the humans were pleased to have them around. One race warming into the other.

But naturally, humans had mixed feelings about their stay. Were they sleeper cells for a grander plan or would they genuinely hold onto their pacifist motives? It was hard to say. These aliens didn't look particularly terrifying. They were slender, towering, had beaming eyes, a pale leathery body and communicated just fine.

Elk, the leader of the aliens had given humans their oaths as tokens of peace. And so all was well. Though the cynical nature of humans ensured that CCTV cameras followed the aliens wherever they went. The aliens, with their superior senses, weren't oblivious to this fact, if it would help the humans to gain their trust, then they needn't violate or bypass these measures.

With their advanced knowledge, they had helped scientists and invariably the world to leapfrog in various fields.

Whereas humanity in turn taught them the finer and frail traits of being human which they so admired.

In daily living in those two cities, they could occasionally be found at the settlements that'd been made for them, also at a handful of functions and at the most recent workplaces that'd become a hybrid of humans, aliens and robots working together to speedily bring forth a better future for everyone into the present time.

For a time, the aliens had helped them make sense of certain obscure things throughout space and time. The two cities they dwelled in saw way more technological development and growth than the rest of the world.

One of the places they had briefly worked at was the observatory in the small town by the lake where Philippa was. She had been one of the most intrigued about the nature of these creatures for all of her life. Her field demanded it. But it was also a natural inclination. Until it passed into normalcy and for a time there was hardly anything startlingfrom space.

* * *

Chapter Two

PATIENT ZERO

"Have you noticed?" she said peering into an infrared radio telescope, "that earth has not been quite the deposit site of space trash for a couple of decades now?"

Pierre only nodded.

She continued, as if introspectively. "Imean. We sure generate a ton of our own trash," she added slyly. Then continued raspingly, "Only that it's shitted back into the planet, not out of it."

Pierre was disquieted. "What the hell

Philippa, why're you talking like this?"

"What the hell? Did you really say what the hell? Pierre? Ouch, don't you understand!"

"I was referring to your voice," he evaded the corrective course she was going to take him on.

She took her eyes off the lens, turnedaround and spoke to him emphatically. "I was wondering why meteorites and asteroids have seemingly forgotten about us." She made a false sulk.

Pierre frowned. "It's been no fun, these decades. I've been reconsidering my career choice for months now, I'll admit."

"In actuality?" She furrowed her brows, almost surprised he might be taking this all for real.

They were leaning against a table.

"I don't wish to die from boredom while on the job. I'm young and unexplored." Pierrewas a tall, tardy and thorough undergrad. He had come from two towns away, leaving his parents and sister behind, to be at the observatory.

She smiled and for a moment looked at the arched perforated ceiling of the observatory. The observatory was conical from the outside. "Only us would talk this way."

"We're bored sick."

"We probably think this is all some plotarc in an uncreative science fiction."

"Bad fiction is fine. What I can't stand is zero sales."

They paused for a second, she jostled his shoulders and then they laughed together.

Together, they watched sundown debut.

The day was done and they'd follow the exit trail to leave the building. The pair made their way through to the large and brightly lit lab. In it there were holograms of RNAs spinning and fridges filled with bacterial samples of probiotic molecules. Amongst other things.

From there, they walked on into an auditorium, obviously meant for lectures. And then they exited the premises.

They had just left the university where Philippa Maxwell was a graduate student at, in the department of astrobiology.

A black, tinted sedan AV was waiting for her outside the gate. She got into it and heaved a resigning sigh, although knowing that the day was not fully assuaged from her. She relished the relinquishing of control this short trip offered; this once, this truly brief moment, she didn't need to be at the fore of her life, charging things forward.

She was routinely offered snacks from the headrest which she found rather unappetizing. She was famished but she'd didn't know it just yet; clouds of thoughts muddled her mind. She also declined to converse with the program about her day or whatever feel-goodnonsense it was programmed to say.

When she was left to herself, she properly slumped in her seat. Time passed illusively and she experienced the stillness of fantasy and like an apt daydream, she arrived at her destination. "Okay," she murmured, pushing herself upwards with her elbows.

The doors automatically flapped open; she found the let out rude. She let herself out of the car and stood outside of the iso-center.

The 'taxi' tab illuminated ever brightly on its roof as it sped off navigating its way and flaunting its vacancy. She stared somberly atthe AV; in reality she was dragging her feet to get into the facility. Scared of what she'd see or hear, perhaps. It was not an unprofessional fear, or the lack of curiosity that clotted in her legs. She was arrested by sentiments instead.

She had been here several times over the past month. Before now, she had occasionally visited the iso-center forresearch. One however didn't need to frequent an iso-center, except for when therewere breakouts in unusual illnesses. Of uncontrollable virality the scale of a pandemic.

That was why the iso-center was located on the outskirts of town.

The night had an arid air to it, as though infested with drowsiness. She saunteredtowards the entrance, flashed her ID at the door, put on her PPE and casually greeted the staff through the hallways and everywhere else she met them, all completely clothed in their protective gears.

She heard the sound of sirens bleating outside as they intermittently arrived in their numbers. She saw the staff creating even more makeshift wards for the unprecedented number of new arrivals. Soon enough, the hallways were no longer hallways but high density treatment spots. So much had changed since the last time she got here.

Phillipa moved around confused, but thrust forward by a tinge of dread to where she started for. Hoping that things would not have changed that much to mislead her from where she knew she was headed, or to have her beg for the assistance of one of these overworked and most likely short-tempered nurses.

She arrived at his ward and he was there, sequestered in a sterile white room with transparent walls. He was unconscious; it was explained to her that that was attempted in order to slow the evolution of the virus in him.

The virus had been speeding up and his condition had been worsening.

The unsaid fact was that everyone was scared of what further stages of the novel virus he'd manifest. RNA predictions had them fearing the worse. So they didn't want to see it, this once, no one was that curious about such a thing. It was simply expedient to have him sedated in an isolation center, thereby postponing the inevitable and simultaneously making what research they could.

She was not told all of that in detail. As a professional, she simply knew it anyway. She looked at him soberly, a tear strode to the surface of her eyes which she wiped off and then watched the monitors attached to him.

The patient was her brother, DannyMaxwell. He'd just turned eighteen. Today was his birthday. And, she thought sourly, he spent it strung up unconscious to a ventilator at an iso-center.

Their parents never got married but Danny and Phil chose to stick together ever since. For a long time they hadn't known the whereabouts of their parents, if they were living or not; if alive, where at all they lived. It was just her and Danny now, they had only each other.

Round the clock, his body's metabolism was being studied. Series of monitors reported such details for them. And currently, she could see two doctors and a nurse through the soundproof walls rustling noiselessly in the room with him, fastened with PPEs and doing some paper and lab work obviously on Danny.

Danny was the source material for most of the stuff at the iso-center. This made Philippa inconvenient even though she knew it was a scientific necessity. She tried to play a hypothetical rundown of his likely activities in her head, to see how he might've contracted the virus.

Why the virus chose her kid brother as its patient zero, she'd never know. She had told a rundown of all she knew about how he spent that day or week and still, nothing.

But she was determined to help however she could. Only that she needed a raft if you will, of intellectual proportions. Some angle to start with, to stand upon, some point to come in through. She felt several hunches but they subsided into nothing. Just trite stuff. She was wallowing in despair and the helplessness that came with being unuseful.

She stayed for a few hours and it'd be around midnight that she'd leave the facility for her home.

The AV came back, dropped her by the edge

of the neighborhood as she demanded. She wanted to stroll home, cogitating. The blocks were scanty and quiet but distractions still abounded. Augmented reality ads popped up from environmentally-friendly trash cans; neon slates beamed from the buildings around and the roads overlayed with moon crust creaked underfoot. For all she cared, it was a dystopian night. The twilight of virulent times, maybe.

Her head had been jumbled lately with her work and her brother's condition -- in an intellectual manner of course. She was seeking ways to augment her work with helping to find a headway for her brother. She looked at the bright words on the beaming beacon spelling the so-called name of her neighborhood projected by a lighthouse across the bleak sky at a trajectory over the buildings. A nighttime routine but another distraction.

She launched herself into the thought of

nighttime skies. Not of extraterrestrials as she'd always done, as if to see behind the cloak of a dark atmosphere. She considered ancient peoples and tried to reimagine how they might've conceived of the world above them; before and after they considered them to be one in the first place.

The pure and free bliss in watching the stars must've had mankind enthralled for all times. Princes and peasants alike. With their heads held high, these skies could have alleviated a great many sorrows for many. And for some it meant hope. Hope for anything. Hope for sentient intelligent creatures that didn't have to spend their livessniffing the ground.

The atmosphere was the known window into the earth. She imagined that at a time, bondsmen and bondwomen, captives, creed-holders and such, must have looked to the skies for hope when they could find none elsewhere.

But what did they hope towards, with so little knowledge of what lay behind those skies?

In truth, it is the nature of hope to be the invisible but viable occupant of one's aspirations in realizing the unknown. That is why we always hope, even when it doesn't make that much sense. Look how hunches and hopes had taken man so far out now into the universe, she thought.

She pulled her eyes from above and fixed them towards the road to be sure that it was empty and she wasn't likely to stumble into anything or anyone. She was right. She rose up her face to see the menagerie of heavenlybodies once again but her conscience, like gravity, briefly smote her and she looked at the ground instead.

Danny is lying unconscious, and you're what, admiring the sky? Every second is supposed to count for him -- you're mean to be helping somehow. The jeremiads in her conscience went on and on. Till she shut it up. "It's night, for goodness sake. Even Danny is resting."

She evaded the guilt-tripping though it managed to deviate her thinking. Her thoughts were mostly terrestrial now. It was the natural, curious thing to do in seeking help from above. But, she reasoned, what if people have been looking in the wrong direction. Yes, they might've been hoping out there as long suspected, but what if that hope was already here?

That theory was toothless. It'd been tried countless times already. She wasn't even sure what she was thinking. She was reasoning more as a speculator than as a scientist. At any rate, some extraterrestrial life form might be the key to a lot of challenges on earth here, she reasoned.

She didn't consider having a grand meetup with aliens and a knowledge exchange, as had been popularized.

What she considered was tinnier, microbial. Too many big distractions in the field were being flaunted already. Almost everything about extraterrestrials was always big, huge, tectonic. So she sought the remote stuff instead.

What if extraterrestrial microbials could hold the answer to certain unanswered questions on earth? Scientists knew how long the list was of universally unanswered phenomena. But right now, all she wanted answers for was the antidote to the virus plaguing her brother's body.

There was one place she could find what she sought. And it was under the oceans. There she'd extract some fresh extremophiles and get to work. Of all the places where extremophiles were now known to abound, she didn't know why she wanted the ocean's. Maybe it was a hunch. She liked to confront and confirm hunches; that was the job.

She sighed resignedly.

She got to her apartment floor, flicked the stripe on her wrist over her door's sensor lock and then she entered her house.

* * *

Chapter Three

THE INCURABLE HUNCH

She prepared herself for a field trip or expedition. She went with a team of three: herself, a pilot and the elated Pierre. They first landed on an aeromedical chopper very close to the lake of the small town they all resided in. The lake was bluish and serene. It wasn't necessarily given to commercial purposes but was largely maintained as a natural habitat and a supportive ecosystem. Miles off the coast of the small town was an ocean as well and the crew hoped to go for it next, should this first mission prove unproductive.

She didn't come here being all too rudderless. She'd learned that the virus had most likely come from water intake. Though no one was sure what specific water source or much less with what to disinfect it with. Water was not something to isolate from the body. But she did just that anyway. She'd been drinking aged or not so recently manufactured soda for weeks on. Pierre simply followed suit. So far, they'd not been infected. Perhaps their strategy was right; but it wasn't to be imposed on everyone anyway. She didn't have any such clout. Not yet.

She had considerable attention on her, being the sibling of patient zero. The world bore a foreboding watch on her, waiting for the symptoms of the virus to set in. She imagined holding their attention for a while because she wasn't planning on getting infected anytime soon, or ever. But at least, whatsoever she did now would sure count. Especially if it was noteworthy stuff. She also knew that most of what she'd attempt, just like now, would come across as rather preposterous to the world. The secret andobsessive life of a scientist was too crazy foreveryone to be allowed to see.

But the attention was a platform she'd need someday, she believed, were she to stumble on something worth the while to tell the world. Something relatable, and not recondite. And for that, she was hopeful something would come off this expedition. Ifshe was being honest, she wasn't all too certain of what they were searching for. All she vaguely knew to be on the lookout for were biosignatures that facilitated life detection.

Pierre echoed her doubts. "What are we

expediting again?" They were in the chopper as it hovered over the lake. They'd been doing this for close to an hour. "Honestly, we're just having outdoor fun, aren't we?" She didn't answer.

"We're here for truth," she said blankly and stared intently at the ripples their rotors were creating on the surface of the lake. Pierre only shook his head in disbelief. He'd never heard such an unscientific answer from her. He knew for sure that science was all about the uncovering of truth and its benefits for us but, professionals just didn't plainly use the word 'truth' to describe these things. It reeked of a philosophical leaning, which was hazardous to a linear, calculated and objective expectation.

"Ready the astrobots," she said to Pierre. He pulled four miniature robots from behind and chirred them to life. Then he let them down below like freed pigeons. The astrobots were robotic drones of two kinds -- the ones with tripod legs and the others bipedal, which were chiefly designed for amphibious reconnaissance.

"What are they to do?" Pierre yelled to her amidst the fluttering wind coming in through the door that'd been glided open.

The astrobots were to descend and scoop the corals and reefs; scraping and searching for molecules, organic compounds that pointed to ancient microbial life. Or abiotic sources of organic compounds. Just about anything weird and worth-noticing would beenough.

"I don't know, maybe just search for strange stuff!"

"Oh, cool! A fun trip!"

They were also to find some alien or mutated form of material, perhaps something that had been prehistorically deposited. And she hoped to reverse-engineer it for use somehow. Well this was what she could do.

The astrobots submerged themselves for hours. Their chopper had landed beside the lake and Phillipa was busy with computations in the meantime, while Pierre was busybodied with the monitors that revealed through the astrobots what was happening below. He was grateful for their having these astrobots. He knew the good old alternative would've been for them to dive in themselves. And it'd have likely been his role. Not when he hadn't overcome his fear of depths.

Hours passed, nothing was forthcoming, nothing striking. Every diver worth their salt had already gone below. If they ever saw anything, everyone would have known. Or maybe not; ordinary divers were not exactly hardcore scientists. Still, nothing novel came through. Philippa was impatient, withdrew the astrobots and declared that they move to the ocean. Pierre had mixed feelings about this. He was scared silly, trapped andsomewhat excited.

They flew out to the ocean to continue the drill. The chopper parked someplace away from the shores and they continued on a sort of hovercraft known as Icestormer. The ocean had been frosty this time of year and the spiky abilities of the Icestormer was ideal to sail through.

When the astrobots emerged onto the surface, they'd been steeped in threads offungi and adorned with mashes of amoeba. For Philippa, it felt like the empty net of a long-toiling trawler. The bearable confidence of a hunch was beginning to give way to unguided skepticism in her.

"Wasn't that what you hoped to find?" They were at the shores, away from where thechopper had landed.

She looked at the astrobots pitiably in her hands and shrugged. "I don't know what's in her." By in here, she referred to the containment the robots carried. Her confidence slowly began to surge, "Yeah, we saw what we saw. And now these decorations. But the bots still scooped up something. Not necessarily remarkable stuff, maybe. Just something."

The day was drawing to its close and the moon was ready to stand sentinel over the night.

"We'll take this back," she said routinely to them, "much to be analyzed in here."

"Sure," Pierre answered dryly. They hopped on the chopper and were on their way back to the lab and then their respective homes.

* * *

Chapter Four

PANDEMIC

They'd spent but a day on the field trip. When they came back, developments seemed to have spun
a week. From the news to social changes, everything appeared to be happening rapidly. A flurry of events were taking place. Society seemed to be reordering itself into chaos. Panic clenched the atmosphere for everyone.

People shopped frantically, sealed their doors abnormally tight, ran berserk, deliriously asked questions and so forth -- all the fictitious signs that the world was ending.

Having caught but the middle of events, all she could see was developments, developments, developments, as reported by the news.

And with such craze, there was no one she'd be asking in person what was taking place all around. She'd have to depend on the news. She stepped into the university's auditorium and used their projector which drew live feed from the internet, to watch the news.

The reporters were themselves remotely corresponding with drone coverage at certain locations of the small town. Fear was so pervasive and no one wanted to risk themselves for anything. Phillipa at once began to consider the claustrophobic idea of being shut up in the lab and observatory for the unforeseeable future. The university premises itself was deserted; whoever remained were grabbing their things to leave immediately.

One thing was clear: the world was reacting to impact. A lockdown of their entire town was imminent She could recognize the patterns. Something had obviously worsened out there. The narrative was coming to what had and she eagerly paid attention. Her gut feeling was morbid.

Deep down, she was dismayed about seeing her brother. She feared that the worse had finally come and he was at the center of it. There was no way whatsoever was taking place wouldn't involve Danny somehow. Seeing Danny again was surely out of the question. It'd become a hazard nobody was stoked about.

The iso-center had been wrecked, it said on the news. Some of the staff had been overthrown and the others killed. Also, the rate of infection of the virus had skyrocketed.

Something fearsome was that scientists weren't sure of the mode of transmission. They had many theories, yes, but all seemed to pan out at the same time and there was yetroom for more. It was known that the origin of the virus was probably waterborne. But how it was propagated from the infected to the uninfected was a mystery. The horrendous mystery no one waited by this time to uncover anymore.

People were pretty much certain that there was no hope whatsoever of a cure. This was because of the transmutation visible in the infected. They had all devolved to the later stages of the virus. The transmutation had setin too quickly and suddenly, as though it hadbeen deliberately triggered. But by whom, was what the nations of the world attempted to answer. Philippa would come back to the politics of the situation just after she'd known what exactly was going on and where Dannymight be.

But for the first time, Danny had ceased to be at the center of the web of things, she heard. Danny not only escaped along with the others, but now he probably caused just as much havoc as them, wherever he was. They now were hordes of them, nameless and in sheer uniformity. It was said that they had transmuted into zombies overnight. One young girl, now hardly identifiable, was brandished by the press as a rare image of the now dispersed physically and physiologicallydistorted victims.

With what Phillipa could see, these newly zombified lot were mindless, gray-eyed, pale skinned and they snorted provocatively. It was a no-brainer that Danny was amongst them, perhaps even leading the pack, she toldherself. There was no looking for Danny, notwithout a cure in hand. A cure she wasn't sure from what quarters it'd emerge from. And clearly, the lengthy and thorough scientific process had already been betrayed by the fast approaching nature of time.

Yesterday would be the last day he'd be called by or considered as Danny. Here on, he was known as a zombie. It melted her heart and she groaned and wept fervently. She clenched her fist, wondering who to be mad at. Someone had got to be responsible for all of this. Now she turned to the politics of the situation.

Nations were pointing accusing fingers at themselves. Searching for who had altered and corrupted nature this much. Politicians were vilifying each other at every turn. There were plenty of blame, conspiracy theories and espionage angles to the matter. All nations distinctively wanted something of their own accord, but this time they agreed it was rather extreme to have one of them covertly introduce such a leapfrogging strategy as this virus.

None was to be saved from it and so a statutory lockdown was imminent. Their small town, where the virus had originated from, was to be thrust into a complete lockdown in about an hour's time. Hopefully, this would contain the spread of the virus and keep the zombies at bay. Everything now made sense that she'd just witnessed in the past hours. The knowledge was truly disempowering for her.

Her survival instincts kicked in and suddenly she made for the building's remote, clasping it in a frenzy, and opted to shut down the doors and windows and any other inlet or outlet for anything at all. Then she waited for the claustrophobia, if it'd come.

The concept of such feat as a solution washed over her once again. She crept forward to hear what the scientists had been doing in regard of a cure, how much progress they'd made. Going full-blown workaholic for this cause right now was the only sane thing to do. Whatever it took, she would join them somehow. She'd help; she softly restated this commitment of hers to herself.

* * *

Chapter Five

THE REBUFF

When she had something good, she'd contact the press for sure.

That was if they didn't contact her first. The lab and observatory had been corresponding with other institutions and scientists from around the world. The selfless and vainglorious ones alike. S-com -- the intranet for scientists, had been overloaded and was on the verge of being jammed. There was so much from her colleagues to sift through. She began to allow herself to believe that breakthrough was looming. And with that enthusiasm came the zest to work longer hours. Into and through the night.

But then there was the mold of doubts to splinter. The necessity of navigating through the ego of other stalwarts, time-tested scientists to be taken seriously. She however trusted that as soon as she managed to have something substantial in hand, such juvenile concerns would be the least on everyone's mind.

She was at the holographic room, modulating and romping on genetic sequencing representations specific to the virus. And then she put together the analysis from the samples that'd been acquired underwater. The veracity of her methods revealed the research was going to be promising. She vaguely hoped to land at something not far off the coasts that virologists had arrived at. But no, she didn't. She extrapolated at something fairly ridiculous. It returned a wave of timidity to her.

How could she show this to anyone, as her big contribution? What sort of nightmarish misadventure this was, she couldn't tell. Yet she consoled herself in the fact that many works of significance didn't always fly at first. But it was risky; she was probably being set up to be the most scornful comic relief of the season.

This was real life where the real grading mattered. And the opposite, well, wasn't necessarily academic failure and disrepute but mostly to be laughed at. She could handle some scorn, she thought to herself. So what the hell. She was going to reach out to the press. She knew what they'd precisely want to hear was news of her having uncovered a vaccine. Such a towering report should've been ideally relayed by a virologist, professor or some other well-paid epidemiologist.

What she had now uncovered were biosignatures of ancient microbial life. It suggested that extraterrestrials might've had a hand in fomenting the virus. It didn't make sense. It was something she had to immediately flush down her mental abyss. So long-winded. It wouldn't just elicit scientific dismissal but political revolt as well.

There was but one alien race on their side of the world, or on the planet, perhaps. Even if they were more, most unprogressive nations were inclined not to disclose them, keeping them as understudied secret weapons. Which they argued, was the historical and intrinsic nature of man, to seek a wonderful amount of advantage over their competitors. To be brutes. To survive.

And so the nations which had opted to embrace and welcome the aliens which they so collaborated with, would've felt seriously spited if Philippa's allegations were true. The head turning towards the aliens, the political and military class immediately they heard that word 'extraterrestrial' was nightmarish. One didn't just wake to accuse a formidable and highly helpful alien ally, she would've been told.

So she had to get past this second obstacle; what was the worse that could take place? Of course, she'd be taking the fall if things didn't go well. Just her. Not Pierre, not the lab, the observatory or the university. For sure the latter would've received some scrutiny afterwards but nothing dire would've come of it. Academic suicide was plausible, if that was what it took them so be it.

Her report was the only pathway she knew to rapidly come up with RNA vaccines. She needed resources and permission to move around. She needed the government on her side, and not to come across as repulsive to them.

Her goal wasn't to cause mass hysteria or whatever. First, she wanted to attract like minds. To assess for whoever would believe in what she did. Just about anyone who'd receive a similar spark or clue or anything it was that made people see possibilities. This would help to speed up the pace of things. In these times that risks abounded, and time was short -- too short to meander the pile of journals, papers and exhibitions on S-com itself -- this was but one of the many risks flying around, a risk worth taking on. She concluded that the only thing at stake was extinguishing herself and right now, it only mattered that she burned brightly if it came to passing out of this world. Only the heat was important. She contacted the press.

As she expected, in a couple of hours she was having more naysayers than collaborators.

The scientific community seemed to have dropped what they were preoccupied with just to criticize and shut her out. Politicians called her theories preposterous. Everything went predictably so. She was the object of jest and ridicule. "I tried something at least," she objected to the fun they poked.

Well as reports swelled, then came a very valuable one. Through the plethora of hysteria and hope, information and cluelessness being peddled on the news, this one stood out. When the aliens spoke, the world always listened. The aliens had suggested through their PR team, that the astro girl, Phillipa, had not been too far off the mark in her theories. The world was taken aback. As the correspondence flowed, they submitted that they weren't sure of whomsoever was behind the virus but that they were onto discovering it and securing the planet for all. Standard PR talk.

She was going to be elated but that was shortly declined. The aliens had further disclosed that they suspected something sinister to be around the corner. They suggested that the promulgation of the virus showed dire signs of the involvement of depraved beings who desired nothing but mayhem on the world. By this time, the virus had grown into a worldwide pandemic. The aliens warned the world to prepare for the next phases that all of this could unfold.

* * *

Chapter Six

ZOMBIFICATION

When the first signs of the virus had appeared, it was being dismissed as being only a variant of some standard ailment. And then it was called something fanciful, and then it was given another classification altogether, atypical to growing medical research. Now it had become a global pandemic which the entire world saw first-hand, except mysteriously, for two cities -- which it was yet to spread into. Families lost each other to the zombification and were never sure if they'd get them back again. The grotesque state of the victims of the novel virus rendered all hope useless for them. How do you reverse something like that; there was only so much a vaccine could procedurally perform.

As per casual scientific advice, the small town first and then the rest of the world was now hooked on to soda. They were all reliving some of what Phillipa had been experiencing lately. It was interesting the rate at which survival instincts kept pace with the adoption ratio of any perceived solution. Like the rest of the world at this point, Philippa was bored and watching. It was on that note she found Danny for the first time after he turned. She saw him on the news. He was at the lake with the hardly recognizable others. It was his brown hair and that forehead akin to the family that zeroed in her recognition of him. She gaped beholding him wearing his zombification. Finally and indeed he was it.

The sense of urgency she felt about everything was now amplified.

It was bizarre the surge of zombies that hung out over at the lake of the small and now forlorn town, like sentinels billowing over some form of water life. They swarmed amorphously like little known species over their conducive hive.

The world was even more curious and watched in real-time augmented reality broadcasts what was unveiled at the lake. It was an intriguing herd behavior to witness. They knew something was to come next, to pop right onto the scene. To know just what it was, was why they all fretfully paid attention. Outsized imaginations ran wild, expectant of what might creep out of the lake; or what these zombies might metamorphose into. Just about anything out of the ordinary was to be expected. It was like seeing the reality TV of the apocalypse.

For the rest of the world, the zombies were

still dispersed in diverse cities. It was old news after all. The lake at the small town wasthe focal point now.

Simultaneously, a crackdown operation was taking place at the two mysteriously protected cities, where the aliens who earlier arrived the planet stayed. They all were being rounded up by the government. The full picture of things wasn't yet uncovered but the government seemed pretty certain that whatever sinister activity was going down, these extraterrestrials had much more to say of the matter than the ignorance they feigned. It was believed that their suspicions of them being sleeper cells was true. The government was determined to find some way to lift such delicate information out of them. They were detained in a high security facility to be interrogated in no time.

Back at the lake, the throng of zombies was starting to give way to something rising up from the waters. Several strangely looking high technology pods swelled up to the surface of the lake. The pods were ash colored, subnormal and ovally shaped. Waterdripped and dissipated from them as theyglided towards the shore. The hermitically- sealed doors whined open.

From them emerged creatures that were twice a man's height, had tawny, leathery bodies, rounded eyes as if sealed into their oblong heads and noses that were nasally interlocked with their mouths, imbued to stream whatever it was that they breathed. They also had small, enclosed hands but with an aperture in-between and mind-reading abilities. They bore an aura of malevolence that made the world realize that their arrival was going to be game changing. They were about forty in number and with extraterrestrial consideration against a lesser advanced species like mankind, that felt like an army. Striding under the sun, theyglistened with unreal colors.

These were the conquest seeking aliens. They were responsible for poisoning the lake first and then other waters around the world.

From their low-orbit undetectable arrival on the earth from their planet, they had penetrated the earth from underneath its southern hemisphere and made their base on the ocean floor.

As they came out, the zombies made an aisle for them from which an awkward procession followed. The order of things became evident. The strength of their intent towards mankind, which was the thought on everyone's minds, was not all too clear. But the subversion of these zombies into becoming their soldiers was most gloomy.

People expected more doom. Even for the entire world to be zombified or killed or worse. World leaders however anticipated a moment of diplomacy, just like when the others had first arrived. There was much to be made sense of. Why were aliens popping up on the planet in this decade? Man had been probing for them for more than a century in the ends of the galaxy and yet there was next to nothing. So why now, what was happening? The leaders believed they could start with these questions at least.

Since the virus had spread to the rest of the globe, in that state of panic world leaders unanimously considered offering up control to the solution-trotting, usurping aliens. They believed control would still be seized anyway. Better thoughtfully than not. But the military might of the world was substantively readied for some form of deterrence or the other. Time was of the essence because their knowledge of these creatures was novel as well. It'd be hard to develop a strategy against them. Everything was being developed on thego.

Shortly, they learned that the aliens soughtto make earth their new home and also furtherother discreet agendas. The aliens moved in earnest. A portentous earnestness.

* * *

Chapter Seven

AN ALIEN SHOWDOWN

The government realized their mistake and rushed to free the other aliens whilst still faking cooperation with the newly arrived ones. The aliens were briefed on the sudden move of the government to reverse their earlier made decision. They prepared themselves as the effective allies that they were, to leave those two cities and make for the small town wherethe newly arrived aliens were at.

Earthlings had started referring to the first alien tribe which had arrived earth as Terrans.

Because they landed on the soil. Then the others were known as Pods, or sometimes The Amphibious. And so it was said that theTerrans were going for the Pods. The world wasn't sure what to expect, not knowing however tricky and dicey the thin line between diplomacy and battle might be amongst extraterrestrials.

The military as a matter of contingency, had promised to act as backup, succinctly preferring this plan where they didn't have to lead the offensive. The army had the small town surrounded from its outskirts. They were also careful to avoid lethal aerial surveillance and operations. Preferring not to incite premature provocation. They bore tranquilizers for the zombies.

The Pods now occupied the small town that overlooked the lake. People deserted the town in their numbers by night until they were stopped. With the ones who remained being tightly shut in their homes, the town seemed like a ghost town. Given that the proximity of the proverbially fallen apple did not lie too further from the tree, the town stayed as the base of the operations of the Pods.

Back at the lake some zombies whom now were all their minions, stayed there to protect their pods and the premises at large so no one dared to come any close to retrieve or interfere with anything. Their unity with the zombies had intensified and they were able to telepathically communicate with them all.

From the small town the aliens pinned themselves to, they hoped to bring the world into submission and had a strategy for that. First, they believed that to get in sync with the consciousness of a race or a people, they had to try out their music -- both past and present. To do so, they accessed the global music database which had been created using AI. Not being fanciful beings, their intent was not to enjoy the melodies mankind danced to. Rather, they sourced for the technical details that underscored different frequencies and notes.

It wasn't all vain because from there on. They educed the gateway to the universal voice command and controls of man. From the command center screen, a sort of code block that looked Tetrislike or like a giant pixel, rearranged itself into an order that opened up everything to them. This allowed them to take control of every and any logistical feature that'd been logged on to the interconnected world. With this, entire national codes and defense protocols were exposed to them which they wielded for their next phase of things.

Before opting for an open assault, the Terrans first tried what was a remote warfare. They tried to gain back control of certain critical infrastructure by hacking into some of what the Pods had taken control of. The Pods resisted these uncanny moves for sure, holding onto and creating more disruptions in the systems under their control.

The move abrupt move left was a direct confrontation of the Pods by the Terrans. The Terrans made their way through into the small town, past pockets of zombie sentinels and made for the university that the Pods had turned into their citadel. For space related reasons, they wanted to initiate the next phase of their plans from there.

They'd hoped to utilize all of the university's space program resources for this purpose. Everything from the observatory to the facilities and space complex. And still, other resources were being imported from different parts of the world for this reason. Rocket and satellites parts, rocket fuel and eminent scientists were being taken for this cause. From all indications, an operation wasin view.

Presently they were at a facility where these parts were being warehoused. Ork, the ferocious leader of the sinister aliens sniffed an unusual scent in the air. He hadn't perceived anything like that since when their ship broke into pods below the ocean. Something so nonhuman. Then the spots from which the scents emanated from kept increasing, moving into place, stalling.

Without turning, he sighed and called outthe first scent he'd sniffed. "Ah, Elk. Good old stalwart. Haven't you got a planet to be on?"

Elk approached. He was taller and more stout looking. "I should have," he said sadistically.

Ork edged into him, facing him head-on atan unappreciable distance and asked him."Why do you defend these pathetic beings?"

"I don't know, maybe it's the coffee and fresh air that's gotten to me."

Fresh air, amongst other things, had been a contender on their planet. Ork and his darktribe of aliens on their home planet had laid waste to much of the planet in their quest to retrieve the treasures of the universe. They drilled and drilled all over the planet seeking for these treasures.

Soon, their extreme efforts made the planet quite unhabitable. Their atmosphere grew porous and their planet's core gushed upwards, exterminating a great number of their kind. Ork and his followers modified themselves to adapt and continue the carnage. Next they moved to other planets in the galaxy to resettle and continue their quests, leaving theirs behind in a wraith of flames.

Elk and the others who'd narrowly survived,

swore vengeance on Ork and his lot for their enormous crimes to the lives of their kin, their planet and the portentous danger they posed to the galaxy at large. But finding them was the first challenge but also not so much of a priority as resettling was. Earth seemed as a fitting option for them and now, it had gifted the Elk tribe with an opportunity to dole out it's vengeance on Ork's.

Ork snarked. "You're growing pathetic yourself. Concerning yourself with the baser elements of this world. Things so base, a significant population of them barely participates in."

"What can I say, fresh air is priceless," he shrugged. And raced in blistering speed with rage towards Ork. Then he leaped up to deal him a head blow.

They clashed mid-air. The impact sent a

vibrational effect throughout the room. And they fell backwards, rolling apart to the ground.

Ork had shot him just in time with a de-energizer, a lazer orb emanating from the aperture of his hands. All Pods had them. As leader, his was the most powerful of all.

Elk staggered to his feet, disdainfully spat a silvery liquid from his mouth, shook off that blow, grunted fiercely, and charged at Ork with blinding speed. He hurled Ork from behind and flung him across the full-length of the room.

Ork fell against the lower wall and rose again like he'd been boomeranged. He came close and they did ultrafast fistfighting. Outmaneuvering each other with their mind-reading abilities, their blows barely touched each other as it destroyed the unmissable things beside and behind them.

The rest of the Terrans, armed with their

guns, swiftly attacked the Pods, roughly matching themselves in number. The aliens, all being capable of jumping to great heights, attacked mid-air and on the ground. Some were unsuccessfully trying to pull out the heads of the opponents; some were trying to lethally break body joints; the rest were flinging themselves around, seeking more and more room for their duel. Speed was important for the Terrans to make the Pods unpermitted to use their de-energizers.

The soldiers began shooting standard bullets. The bodies of these aliens were virtually impenetrable. So what brave ones they were among them had to go for fistfighting, collaborating with what Terran had already engaged any of the Pods. The men climbed on the backs of the Pods, staggering them as they jerked about and stifling them however they saw fit.

But they still wouldn't be subdued. For many of the humans who had attempted this,the Pods flew horizontally, effectively ramming their bodies into whatever hard object it came against. These and many other fatalistic moves made sure that many of such soldiers died. The casualties on the human side was on the rise.

Meanwhile, Ork and Elk still battled it out. Ork was slammed with a great thud to the ground, cracking through two floors. There he wheezed and began to telepathically call for his new minions the zombies, to come help upend the advantage of the Terrans.

They had previously equipped them with lethal guns, infused with outworld properties and capable of stunning aliens.

Innumerable guided bullets began glinting all over the premises, bypassing objects and striking forcefully at the Terrans.

It was an all-out clash, a festival of violence. And it spanned the entire grounds of the university. There was hardly anywhere free from it, as the environment gave them more than enough room to do battle as they as they saw fit.

Just then, Phillipa was sneaking into the battle scene from the observatory, to salvageher brother Danny.

* * *

Chapter Eight

CONTROL FREAK

She could hear the resonance of the battle going on over at the storage facility and then broadening out to the rest of the school. She incisively felt the clutches of death upon hearing the thudding snd clanging noises from across the school. Tonight, was one lousy undertaker into the realms of death. She breathed its pungent presence in the air and did her best within her racing heart to ignore it. Focus Philippa, focus, she said to herself. All of this was highly unusual and strange for a theoretician.

She had witnessed chaos before but, always at some molecular scale. Never at this life-sized scale. Moreover, she'd always only been an observer of such things. Never one tobe quite caught in-between all of this. And the night was endless, frighteningly stretching itself against the dawn of day. This limited her movements, her escape. But then she had a thought, to vast even more illumination out of the night. To switch off the lights. It was what she believed any normal and yet insanely frightful human would do. Take out the lights and you're free. She had to make for the power room.

She was at the lab and it'd take several hallways for her to get into the power room. There was a mapping screen that told her so -
- the one dimly lit thing she allowed in the lab. The whole lab was pitch dark, throwing out

every visible clue of a human presence in there. So far, it proved to be effective. She judged that it'd be relatively so for the entire premisses if she could just do this one brave thing tonight.

She began slouching and crouching through the hallways. Here the screams and moanings were more intense than she'd previously imagined. She could literally hear people and beings dying. Sometimes she froze with fear and other times when the locomotion returned she does up her crawling as fast as she could. It was all a start-stop process, progressive all the same.

As she passed the hallways and corridors, she saw the walls of certain rooms having been smashed and enmeshed into bent sheets. Just then, she cringed and lowered her head, dodging the murmuring and subsequently lifeless body of a soldier that was thrown her way unknowingly. She paused and looked at his ruptured neck, his tongue protruding from his mouth and his face blackened from burns.

She shivered and continued, just a turn left up ahead would lead into the power room.

When she entered the room, she went for the detrimental switches. She pushed it off with her full might. The entire university gradually went dark and for a second those who did battle paused to absorb what had just taken place. Not deterred by this at all, their fighting continued.

Since the zombies had arrived from wherever it was they'd been quartered, the advantage had tilted in favor of the Pods. Terrans had to take shield from the guns the zombies wielded. More soldiers were slain in the crossfire whilst taking down zombies with them. The number of zombies kept increasing in every corner of the scene where the battle took place. The soldiers were outnumbered and a fallback was not to be forestalled. Subtly but swiftly, the remaining soldiers alive pulled out of the scene for their own safety, seeing that they were outmatched with little to nothing else to do here.

Terrans determined not to critically harm the former humans which now we're zombies. This carefulness of theirs was predictably thought to be a weakness by the Pods. And even worse, an advantage to be fully exploited by them. The zombies were their most aggressive arm of the fight while the Pods came in the second flank.

Some spots at the back, amidst the rest of the fighters, Ork maintained his direction for Elk. Ork's eyes were set on Elk from across him and Elk's conversely so. They now were outdoors and freed from the shackles of the enclosure. Between them was the struggle of their comrades.

Ork was ranting about the rationale of his outlandish ambitions. He spoke of his right to dominate the universe and tilt it in the direction it ought to go.

"There's a word for that out here, Ork."

Ork widened his eyes, anticipating the answer.

"It's called a control freak. It's always so. One madman per millennium," he said with his croaky voice.

Ork rushed at him. Elk slid past him at knee level, thrashing his kneecap while at it. Ork fell to the ground on his knees and Elk came before him, towering above him. Ork looked destitute of mercy. Elk's mercy. Elk had his gun pointed at his neck, perhaps waiting for his surrender. "It's a shame I didn't have this opportunity on our planet, you would never have gotten here. I would've gloriously chopped you in bits," Elk said the words grittily. Ork knelt quietly, hoping for a liberating disruption from any point on the battlefield.

Ork was telepathically drawing the most vicious zombies out to come encircle Elk and take their shot at exterminating him. He wore a sneer and coughed ringlets of substances. Cheerful over the idea that Elk was soon to be surrounded. Elk's senses picked the coarse scent of zombies so close to him, their gazes and weaponry fixated on him. It was obviously his turn to surrender if he so pleased. He'd been locked into their target and could see the laser dots roaming erratically about his body. He strapped his gun to his back, held up his hands to fake a surrender and in an instant jumped away from them, escaping the firing they immediately initiated.

Retreating himself, Elk ordered the rest of his tribe and any soldier who might've been left on their side, to all fallback, retreat and regroup.

Ork displayed what was analogous of a smile; being pleased with watching those antagonists flee. He turned around and looked at the wreck they'd all made throughout their wrestle. He hoped some of their most critical infrastructure, critical to the space program they wanted to continue, hadn't been irreparably damaged. He sent his minions, subordinate aliens, to go assess things all over. Particularly at the complex and storage facilities.

* * *

Chapter Nine

THE BAIT

Phillipa was unsure what was currently taking place; she heard no wild noises of blows being exchanged, strange weapons emptied or the bellowing sounds of dying beings and rallying ones alike. She heard nothing but the creaking and thumping sound of broken objects finally letting themselves to the ground, she felt the risen temperature in what the likely aftermath of things or maybe an intermittence. She also heard the soft combustion and crackling sound of metallic things that's been made somewhat molten by rapid and intense firing.

The abrupt cessation of the violence trickled a new kind of fear in her. What exactly was going on anyway? Were they alldead? Had they somehow managed to cancel each other out? She caught between excitement and dread. If the aliens had all died, frankly she believed it to be a good thing, for the greater good at least. If they were alive and conceivably here up to negotiating things out as sane things, then we'll, all wasn't quite lost. Or perhaps it was none of those. This foreboding silence could've been just about her. No wait, perhaps they were taking care of an execution and soon would continue the fight. Maybe it was Danny who was about to be executed? His insubordinate and rebellious side could have risen to the fore and caused unforeseen distress for the Pods. Now they would want him dead. That obviously meant that their side had lost and they were doing nothing more than licking their wounds. That was why this silence permeated the atmosphere. Itmade such unproven sense.

She rose and hopped towards the observatory. Going through the hallways, she could hear footsteps rustling against the ground apparently browsing for something. Likely for survivors and eavesdroppers and courageous journalists (none of which were present), she thought. She moved in the most surreptitious and stealthy way she'd ever done. Her life literally depended on how lite she able to allow her breath, feet and heartbeat flow. This was the greatest experience of control she yet had to pull in her life.

Two Pods had just passed into a room adjacent to the wall she leaned behind. It was a narrow escape for her. For a second she considered all the awful things they could've done to her, had they found her there. She would've totally been a recipient of the wrath that came from their loss. A loser's vengeance, especially on a lower form of being, could only carry untold devastation.

She moved into the next room and sighed in relief or what was a momentary celebration of the opportunity to breathe once again.

Then she started for the hallways, nimble-footed and inauspiciously anticipating that random moment when she'd be caught. But she wasn't.

She finally sneaked into the observatory her initial destination. There she hoped to take the most important peek of her life, into the telescope. Panicky, she alternated it to make sure its trajectory was over the school, and not space. She was going to find Danny through its powerful lenses and possible, it sure should be possible, she'd save him. He'd been recognizable once, he should be again.

She thrust the telescope another way and zoomed into the direction of the initial fighting scene. Then elsewhere. Them someplace else. She saw Ork -- his menacing look even from backwards, frightened her eyes away from those lenses.

She summoned the courage once again to peek. She found some zombies, scanned each of them thoroughly. These set had blood splattered on their faces, making their facial features obscure their identities. She determined that Danny would hardly be among these ones that'd now become brutes. She turned again to search for Danny before the door of the observatory got barged into.

Two aliens had picked up her scent. "You, human. Come right here!"

She twirled around the room, plotting an escape. They easily caught onto her, grabbed her by the shoulders and made away with her. She shrieked and jerked to free herself from their grasp but to no avail. Her legs her aloofthe ground.

She was brought to where the leader of these aliens, Ork, was. He seems pleased to see her. He at once recognized her for who she was: an individual with invaluable ties toeverything.

"Ah, Philippa," he said. "Nevermind how irreverently these loyal soldiers are holding on to you. It is because of your importance inall of this. You do know this."

Danny strode forward. He came closer to her and sniffed. His consciousness did not record any memory of her whatsoever. She felt most hopeless and more despondent thanever before. She'd pictured that Danny would somehow inflict a contravention that'll splurt her out of the hands of these aliens, before she'd perhaps be abducted further into wherever else it was, or even outer space.

"You are sister to patient zero. Our portal to domineering this world. Did you try to save him, hmm?" Ork taunted. "How hard did you try at the lake?" He held up her face in disgust. "That's right. Not hard enough." He threw back her face, "Take her away." He moved over to oversee the components the other aliens had brought in for the space program they were working on.

In the dark, the eyes of these aliens beamed brightly and emitted ultraviolet-like rays. They moved around refitting the tickets and satellites and seeing to what modifications they could achieve.

They had Phillipa enclosed in a room, bolted and encrypted with additional security from the outside. She wasn't a priority and yet they weren't sure what to do with her. They knew someone would come for her, as part ofstandard human protocols. They weren't sure what kind of leverage she'd serve to be though. They didn't see her s one anyway. That was why they shut her in that old relegated room and moved on with their priorities.

* * *

Chapter Ten

THE COERCION TREASURE

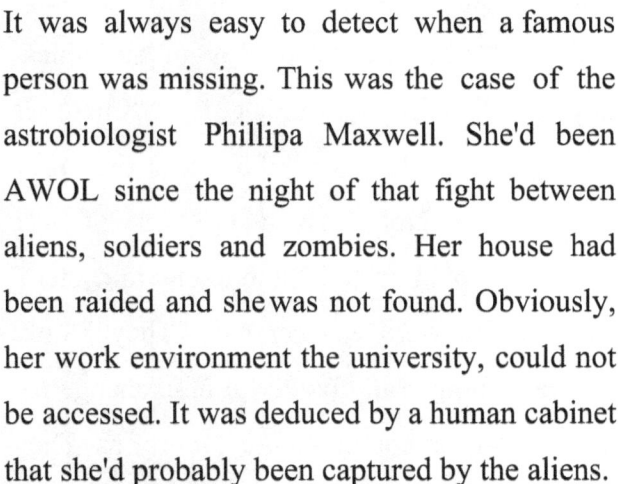

It was always easy to detect when a famous person was missing. This was the case of the astrobiologist Phillipa Maxwell. She'd been AWOL since the night of that fight between aliens, soldiers and zombies. Her house had been raided and she was not found. Obviously, her work environment the university, could not be accessed. It was deduced by a human cabinet that she'd probably been captured by the aliens.

The Terrans got wind of the news and the plot to retrieve this invaluable human in the custody of the other aliens was underway.

The humans had their own independent plan to recover her. Devoid of alien participation. Spearheaded by their bestdiplomatic strategies.

Terrans made the humans understand the terms of the Pods non-existent negotiation strategy. No matter the quality of tactfulness they employed, it wouldn't fly. "There is nothing that belongs to the earth that they would want. Not even a prisoner of war exchange would suffice," the aliens told them. The humans were exasperated. "They'll only take something really powerful in exchange for her. And we cannot let her die. Not for us. They ultimately want us out of the way."

Another showdown was impending.

The Terrans clearly didn't hope to win. It was not a battle over their many contentions.

They only wanted to create a scenario of disarray where Philippa could escape; this should've been easier than a win or lose battle.

Elk came to the rescue. He appeared to be quite thoughtful and would speak predeterminedly on what next was to be done. He knew what next should be done. It didn't have to outrightly involve the humans. It was matter-of-factly exclusive to their intellect. He determined that the aliens would themselves see this to its end. He could read the desperation on the minds of the human cabinet and hopeless they were getting.

First he regarded their losses of the aliens, their headcount, noting by how much they'd been depleted. The is would entail what sort of strategy they'd be able to deploy.

They were roughly half their original number that remained. Aliens were capable of living for a very long period of time -- for centuries and up until over a millennium.

Never before had their extinction been so brought into question. And now it was possible that they'd be left in the recesses of the clouds and dust of the solar system -- only to be studied as the remnants of an arcane junk in space. As did their old and former planet, squashed and disintegrated into innumerable asteroids and fodder for comets. That was in the aftermath of the Pods, what's they'd done to the inappreciable planet in the end.

Elk was calculating the likely outcome things would take. This could be their last stand in the universe. The idea of giving their lives for this cause didn't seem too farfetched. It was expected to be a suicidal mission. But whatever attempts they stretched to make would be better off than the seductiveness pacifism was posing.

There was much more at stake, monumentally orchestrated to ruin the universe itself. The aliens weren't merely to be involved in this potential mission becauseof the captured astrobiologist alone. Theyalso needed to paralyze and terminate the acceleration of the space program the Pods were developing. They knee that for sure the Pods intended to launch an all-out and widerrange of attack and domineering over theuniverse. And if with any luck, they would seek to acquire the treasures of the universe and decimate this galaxy and move on to another till they were at the rim of the universe.

But first, the Terrans knew that these Pods weren't done with the earth per se. They agent just arrived to enfeeble the earth and use it asa launch pad for their next moves. Instead, they worried that all that they saw so far might've only been a detour. A concealment of the main event, if there was one. As far as domination goes, there could predominantly be but an all-powerful, ultimate and supreme plan -- the one which they'd been witnessing. But if there was to be more, which was entirely possible, it was only a matter of a handful of menacing hours before whatever evil they were up to would certainly come to pass. So a quick offensive was the sure way to go.

The fate of the world depended upon it. The state of the planet was going to devolve even further. The pandemic was but the first if more than a dozen plagues the Pods could've had coming.

For the Terrans, they'd fight for the virtues of mankind they'd come to slowly imbibe. The Pods on the other hand would be out there and everywhere for universal conquest. There was one which the Pods hellishly desired to overthrow -- the supreme leader of the universe, the protector of the treasures of the universe and one whose rule of offering a dualism to life -- a system of choice – greatly angered Ork and his followers who desired as superior species, to thrust the universe towards a single, unbroken and undivided fate.

The Terrans went to the university and found Ork and his minions at a complex that hadn't been too disturbed from the former violence. There they had a confrontation and it was most visible how that the Terrans were highly outnumbered. In order not to initiate the first move that'll permanently cause them to withhold Phillipa for as long as possible, they opted for a negotiation first, for her freedom. Their opening position was outrightly rejected by Ork. Then he went on to dole out tirades about how disgustful this gesture of the Terrans was. "And what," he continued, "they call you

'Terrans' like you're some sort of land animal."
Ork chortled. "Whereas Elk," he said emphatically, "you can rule the universe alongside with us."

"You don't rule the universe," Elk responded definitively.

"Oh, yes." He tapped his head as if something had clicked in it. "I don't. Not yet."

"Not ever, trust me."

"Because your supreme leader, your very much defeatable leader does?"

"You know you first have got to get out of earth alive, don't you?"

Ork stood back and chuckled. "I know what this is. You're outnumbered and outwitted. You're out here talking tough to deflate uncourageous spirits, none of which are present among us. You simply cannot eviscerate our agenda."

"We sure can purge life from you." "Give up
and give in," he shrugged.

"Depends on who does first." He moved
into position and they oscillated themselves.

"Tell me, where is Phillipa? She's not a part
of this."

"You know she is. And I must say, I like the
idea." Elk goal was to tempt Ork and flaunt an
irresistible offer before him. Something that'll
stop him in his tracks. With that, he'd uncover
tidbits of information on Philippa's state of
being. He'll have leverage. But what was next to
be done with that leverage was something else.
He knew if this exchange were to assumptively
go through, it'd somehow serve to slowdown
next steps to follow, if there was any.

But it was counterintuitive to make this

exchange; it'd be handing Ork the world without a sweat, after all this while. It didn't make that much sense. It didn't need to currently make sense.

"I've got something that you'll need," he said to Ork. "Something you've been searching for, for centuries on. Just free Philippa first."

"Hold on a second. I am curious. Why is this mortal important to you?"

"What's power compared to life?" he shrugged. "I get it, you'll never know."

"You used to have an idea of these things. But now, you've been sapped, old stalwart."

"Hand the girl over," Elk demanded, fixating his fingers at Ork.

"How am I not sure your minions are up and about, raiding the premises for her? This might we'll be a stealing exercise than an exchange."

"We've tried that. We couldn't find her. Give her up."

"What have you got?"

"One of the treasures of the universe."

Ork looked at him, skeptically searching his face. "It can't be."

"How do you think the two cities we reside in were able to stay unaffected by yourvirus?"

"Sounds plausible. So where is it right now?"

"Close. The girl first." Ork gestured to oneof the aliens on his side to bring forth the girl. It took a few minutes and she was presented before Elk, held tightly by the arms and fettered into an unworldly yoke about her legs and neck.

"Your turn. Bring out the treasure, stalwart."

Elk reluctantly asked for a box from one of the aliens on his side.

"So...you are just going to hand it over to me. No tricks?"

"I am handing it over," he held it before his face.

"Tell me, what is inside?"

The box was ancient and plain. "Power," he answered balefully. "The coerciontreasure. You want it, don't you?"

"Give it at once," his eyes glittered with lust.

"The girl first." They passed her along to Elk. He took her and placed her securelybehind him and stood statued. He was telepathically depositing really visual bits of information in her mind. In actual time it all felt like a brief moment when he was done. She cringed with the floor of understandableknowledge.

"You can have it." He threw it over the hostile distance between them. Ork greedily caught it and sighed hoarily.

It was under no circumstances that Elk would permit his usage of the coercion treasure. The coercion treasure by design, when it was activated, was capable of making request of the bearer. The outcomes were unlimited and would span across cities, states, nations and continents -- it would be an unprecedented compulsion like the world had never before seen.

Elk zapped at Ork with this head at his chest level just he was about to flip open the box. Together, they travelled across the space in the room and crashed on a wall at the other end. Instantaneously, a fight erupted between the rest of the aliens. Elk knew this was it, the fight they wouldn't win. But it'd be better if they went down fighting. Perhaps it'd inspire and overturn the much sedated humans to do something inspiring. And even if it didn't, it'll all make a good story someday anyway. They fought on and on with that conviction.

* * *

Chapter Eleven

THE FATE TREASURE

In between all of this, Phillipa had been freed, her yoke torn asunder. She evacuated the university, stealing a car and making for one of the cities where Terrans lived. She caught the flurry of thoughts she was having, determining that a hyperloop would be a better and ultrafast means of transportation.

She ran through deserted streets, sensitive sidewalks laced with space tourism ads and across decaying flowers and overgrown lawns and gardens. She made for the lair of the Terrans in that very city and rummaged the building for a specific artifact. A box. She'd know it when she see it. She'd seen it before -- but not exactly -- she'd had a trance where it was so visually featured. The trance that'd been planted in her head by Elk just before he let her go, moments after he received her from Ork.

She found the doorway behind where the artifact was securely and obscurely stored. Not even world governments knew of it's existence. Phillipa was the first human being to not only know of but handle the fate treasure, the second of the treasures of the universe given to the Terrans by the supreme ruler of the universe.

She opened the box, still following the premonitional instructions given to her by Elk's trance. Inside of it was a blue glowing orb with a jellylike and ethereal quality. As she reached out for it and held it, the glow reached further up her arms and body. Her hands turned it rightwards in the box and it's effect came into play.

It bestilled the ambience of the world. In a split second, the trend of things was juggled, altered and reordered. The events of the past few weeks and months were rewinded and reversed. And here was the all-important part: she was able to intertwine and mingle her mind, her consciousness, therein tooling the fate treasure to how she wanted the actual fate of recent times to turn out.

Everything went back to the dawn before the virus. She could see it all in a trancelike state; there she excluded the evil aliens from ever conceiving an intent on the earth, deleting their footprints from time and flinging them into some other hopelessly remote, far-flung and cold planet right in another distant galaxy entirely.

These were the new outcomes -- a prosperous and desirable fate; for all of mankind and the universe at large. One that had them oblivious to the astronomical events that had taken place before their eyes and trampled on their very lives most recently. In this blissful ignorance, they continued the activities of their daily lives.

In regular times when she'd come across Elk (the aliens still retained the memory of l that'd transpired recently), she asked him out of curiosity if he had always known that the virus had extraterrestrial origins. He responded in the affirmative, stating that their policy of non-interference emailed that the humans had to come to their own realizations and conclusions by themselves. For he said, their fate has always been in their own hands, to direct as they saw fit.

Other Books by the author:

"120" Dylan called while walking into the field. He wore khaki shorts and a white T-shirt. His muscles flexed as he walked, and his jaw ticked while his fist clenched and unclenched. Nobody had ever been this bold before and he was getting impatient to find this girl who had him riled up so badly. "I'm here" The line of slaves parted revealing 120. Her thick raven black hair was braided on one side while the unbraided part fell on her shoulder. Her skin glistened with sweat. She moved slowly through the path the slaves created. Her bold steps were unwavering under Dylan's unnerving stare. She stopped directly in front of Dylan, staring him square in the eye before making to speak. "I... went out for some air" She said. "You went out for some air? With whose permission, slave?" He spat, disgust dripping from his tone. "I am no slave. Just a girl you've held against her will". Loud gasps of shock were heard as all the slaves were surprised. "And, I have a name. My name is Vivien not 120' She stated with her head held high.

Naif@naifbooks.com

www.ingramcontent.com/pod-product-compliance
Lightning Source LLC
Chambersburg PA
CBHW030556130626
46552CB00006B/2574